The Sapiosexual Submissive

An Erotic Romance

Ronda DeMure

ISBN: 978-1-63786-003-8

Sex pleasure in woman is a kind of magic spell; it demands complete abandon.
— SIMONE DE BEAUVOIR

CONTENTS

1 NATURAL SUBMISSIVE

The on line conversations over the past couple of weeks which had resulted in this coffee shop meeting ran through Lydia's mind as she sat waiting at the table, looking for him through the picture window. His name was Duncan and he was an experienced dominant, whereas she could best describe herself as not even a neophyte submissive, merely a curious wannabe. Single since her divorce years ago her life nowadays was mostly occupied with work, and since she enjoyed her business successes and had no wish to be married again she was here with a hope to explore a long time curiosity that might fill the increasingly gnawing void in her life. The conventional world of dating certainly had not. With its superficial conversations and focus on the trivial, dating regular people was as unstimulating as the unimaginative sex that went with it, and after so many attempts she had decided to give up on it. Instead, she had decided to take a foray into the world of submission and dominance since there was a refreshing honesty to be had in a relationship where the focus was to be on a shared fetish. At least, she hoped so.

Duncan had been unique on line, asking few questions about her physical appearance but wanting to learn as much as she could tell him about her fantasies and desires. She had no specific activity in mind, she knew far too little to even speak intelligently to that, but from her reading erotica she knew how she wanted to feel. She wanted to be helpless and disconnected, and she longed to experience the curious balance that existed between pleasure and pain. Duncan seemed to know what she meant in spite of her vagueness, and through their email correspondence he had already helped her to understand herself a little more in this regard. He had also explained to her how submission may induce a state where all that exists is feeling the moment, and in this subspace one can experience the most exquisite orgasms imaginable. She wanted that experience, but the realization that she would probably be willing to do just about anything in exchange for it was a bit terrifying. Was it even possible that somebody could actually possess that level of control over her?

Duncan had been a dominant all of his life, but he kept these proclivities in a compartmentalized, secret other life. Twice divorced, he had learned that his needs were too strong to be subjugated to convention, but neither could they be understood by the majority of the world and were toxic to traditional relationships. He placed a high value on monogamy, but the strength of his inner demons had often overridden his values.

He owned a successful brokerage business and was very active with chambers of commerce and service clubs; to the outside world he was a pillar of the community and it was important that the world always viewed him that way. As a result, he employed a careful screening process in his search for submissive partners, but his needs went beyond simply maintaining discretion. Most of the submissive women he had encountered over the years were focused on specific activities, which he was more than delighted to participate in with them, but after a scene he generally found that all he had in common with them was the shared kink. Duncan had learned to accept the revolving door nature of these encounters but was continually on the lookout for that submissive who might also be his intellectual counterpart whom he could have an actual relationship with.

The philosopher Hegel stated that all relationships depended upon differences of power, which was intuitively obvious in the real world, but the conclusion arrived at when one follows that thought is that the most solid relationship would therefore be one akin to master and slave. Such was the reasoning that prompted Duncan to search for the perfect submissive, because finding her would mean he could have a truly authentic relationship. This would satisfy his needs, and he could then happily spend the remaining 95% of his life in the conventional world around him. His logic was impeccable.

Lydia had aroused his curiosity in text, and he was looking forward to see if she would turn out to be the same person in the flesh. An intellectual natural submissive would, indeed, be a gem.

She spotted him walking towards their rendezvous, precisely on time. He wore a dark blue business suit with a colorful silk tie and polished black shoes that matched his leather belt. She was dressed casually in a pink cashmere cardigan and a pleated skirt; per his online instruction, even their attire was to be consistent with the imbalance of power he had so eloquently described to her. In her mind she had equated him to a college professor, so she decided to dress collegiately; he was the authority figure, and she took great comfort that her role would be to simply respond to him.

Their conversation flowed easily and progressed from the obligatory small talk about their respective jobs to their inner desires before they had even finished their first cups of coffee. He explained that a true dominant monitors the submissive to ensure her comfort, but a submissive always has the ultimate control over the situation with something called a safe word, the uttering of which terminates an activity.   She asked if he had ever had a safe word used with him, and his telling her that he had not pleased her tremendously. Very quickly at ease with him and anxious to learn more, she eagerly accepted his invitation to follow him to his house to continue their conversation in a more private setting.

The second cups of coffee they enjoyed together were cappuccinos that Duncan made with his home espresso machine, and they sat on opposite sides of the coffee table in his living room while they drank them.   Lydia relaxed on the black leather couch while he sat on the matching armchair watching her expressions as they talked. "The first step is for you to be comfortable," he told her.

"I feel very comfortable with you," she confirmed, then immediately smirked into her coffee cup at her boldness; excitement and curiosity were clearly overriding any trepidation.

"Splendid," he said and leaned back in his chair. "So since you're also looking warm after drinking coffee, let's have you even more comfortable. Take off your top."

Lydia returned the cup to its saucer and began to unbutton her cardigan; his calm demeanor made it unthinkable to not do what he suggested. She placed her top across the arm of the couch and sat up straight to show off her floral brassier to him.

"That's a very pretty bra."

"Thank you."

"Stand up."

"All right." Lydia stood up straight and pressed her legs together to help conceal any signs of her nervousness.

"Tell me, Lydia, are you wearing stockings or pantyhose?"

"Thigh-highs." She smirked.

"That's good," he gave a quick nod. "I require a submissive to always present with naked thighs. Lift up your skirt for me."

Lydia instantly reached down for the hem of her skirt and raised it past her waist, watching for any sign of approval on Duncan's expressionless face as she held it up while his eyes examined her naked thighs between the tops of her black stockings and her black lace panties.

"You have very nice legs."

The compliment warmed her. She was already so aroused, and yet he hadn't even touched her.

"However," he teasingly wagged his right index finger at her. "Since your panties and bra don't match, one of them has to go. So, let's have you posing topless."

As Lydia unfastened her bra it occurred to her that he wasn't actually ordering her to undress, but she was doing so at his suggestion because she wanted to please him. She placed her bra across the top of her cardigan and lifted her skirt up again, pointing her elbows away from her body so her arms didn't obscure his view of her breasts. The years had morphed the slender 30Bs from her youth into full womanly 32Cs, but she was proud that they still retained their shape and firmness. The areolas almost matched the brunette of her shoulder length hair and her stiffening nipples were betraying the excitement that was also contributing to the growing dampness in the crotch of her panties.

Lydia's unquestioning compliance and her most evident arousal from these simple activities pleased Duncan tremendously by confirming his suspicions from their emails that she might, indeed, be a natural submissive. A woman with such a mindset could be the one able to provide him with the depth of passion that he craved, provided he was successful in uncovering her desires and subsequently facilitating their fruition. Since she had no idea what they were or where they might lead her, she presented as a blank canvas for him to deftly create his masterpiece. If she did turn out to be a natural submissive, then with proper nurturing he would progress her to the point where she would do anything that he wanted. The benefit she would receive in return would be his guidance into, and protection through, the elusive otherworld of subspace.

He permitted a smile onto his face and extended his right hand to her, bringing her around the table to the side of his chair, and then sat her on his lap. "How are you feeling?" He asked, sliding his hand up her skirt to rest on the inside of her soft left thigh.

"I feel absolutely wonderful," she gushed while involuntarily parting her legs as Duncan's fingertips lightly brushed against the front of her panties. "And since you've already given me my safe word, I'm quite ready for my introduction." He had previously told her that when she was ready he would begin slowly with her, and that there would be frequent conversation with the opportunity for her to ask questions. Right now, she felt more than ready for whatever was about to happen next, even though she had no clue as to what that might be. It was unbelievable, but she already trusted him.

He pulled her into a hug and slowly whispered, "Then I'm going to put you across my knees, pull down your panties, and I'm going to spank you," into her left ear.

His whispering caused her body to become limp, which made it easy for Duncan to position her across his lap. He placed his left hand across her back to secure her while gently rubbing her bottom through her skirt with his right. He began with light, even slaps but soon made them a little harder as he slid his left hand to the back of her neck to determine that she had no flinching responses. He then lifted her skirt across her back and caressed her bottom through her panties before proceeding with more moderate slaps, increasing the intensity until he could feel slight tremors from her upper body. "I think you like this," he said cheerfully. She was responding well thus far, so he slid her panties to mid-thigh in order to properly spank her. What happened next would tell him a lot about her potential suitability.

He roughly massaged her already rouge buttocks until she began to murmur, and then brought the flat of his right hand down with an audible smack. Her head rose slightly, but she dropped it down again instantly and he could now hear her breathing. Left hand securely on the back of her neck, he then delivered a dozen more evenly spaced slaps across either side of her buttocks with his right hand. His hand was now tingling and he rubbed it against the heat from her beautifully glowing bottom before moving it down between her legs. The ease with which his fingers slid between her swollen pussy lips was as intoxicating to him as it obviously was to her. He slid his thumb onto her engorged g-spot and latched two fingers onto her excited clitoris and began to slide them back and forth. Lydia screamed into wild orgasm, causing him to move his left hand across her back again and lean forward to keep her from falling off his lap while he continued to provide her with her release.

Slowly withdrawing his hand, he waited until her shuddering settled and then effortlessly rolled her over and cradled her in his arms as he leaned back into his chair. Her large, wet brown eyes conveyed tremendous gratitude before she buried her tear soaked face into the nape of his neck, and he simply held her like that, nuzzling into her hair, until her normal breathing resumed. Duncan was delighted, this had been a most encouraging session indeed, and looking into her eyes when they emerged again, he felt compelled to kiss her.

"That was absolutely incredible," she told him. "I've never been spanked before. It turned me on so much, and then when you touched me, wow."

"And I'm very pleased with you, Lydia." He stood her up and walked to the bar across the room, poured two glasses of mead, and handed one to her. "Here's to you," he said and clinked the rims together. "I believe you're quite a natural submissive." He beckoned to the couch and they sat there side by side.

"I certainly came hard," she confessed, "almost as soon as you touched me."

"The spanking warmed you up nicely. As I said before, I believe that you may be a natural."

"But I feel so selfish now," she smiled as she bit her lower lip. "What about you?"

"Today is all about you, Lydia." Duncan peered at her over his glass; this was exactly how he wanted her to feel. "I want you to go home and email me your thoughts when you have them composed, for I imagine right now they are very muddled."

"You can say that again," she laughed. "So, you're not going to want to, um, fuck me?"

"Not today, no," he responded, smiling at her confusion. "But don't you worry. If you do decide you'd like to take the next step there will be plenty of such activity down the road."

Duncan desperately needed to masturbate as soon as Lydia left. Her submission and spanking been an incredible turn-on for him, and she also had a pleasing body, but it was important that she left with the feeling that she had received far more than he had. Besides, if she really was as intrigued as she appeared to be, he would have her soon enough. Right now the decision to proceed was entirely up to her, and he would await her email.

2 SILK TIES

Lydia's email arrived late in the evening and it contained exactly what Duncan wanted. In addition to thanking him for making her feel so relaxed initially, and then feeling so good during and after her spanking, she expressed an almost fevered desire for more, writing that she would be so grateful if he would help her further explore her submissive nature and accept her willingness to do whatever he wanted in return. He smiled at the delicious innocence of her offer while his cock pushed against the inside of his pants. The email also invited him to her house for dinner, an invitation he graciously accepted. It pleased him that they would also be enjoying food and conversation in addition to the beginning of her training; not only did Lydia appear to be an excellent prospect to be his submissive, but he was already imagining the potential for an intellectual relationship with her too.

Her quick response to his acceptance of her dinner offer included asking him how she should be dressed. He immediately sent a message back to her telling her she was to not wear anything at all, and also told her that he would bring the wine. "And there will be an appetizer just for you," he muttered to himself after the email had been sent.

Lydia had been eagerly anticipating his arrival, yet when the bell rang she rather gingerly opened the door, a conflicted mixture of excitement and trepidation flooding her overly stimulated brain. That he had come from his office and was fully dressed in a business suit while she was standing in the hallway completely naked nicely underscored her submissiveness, but her nervousness was also evident. This was not unexpected, however, and before they had even exchanged any words Duncan pulled her to himself, holding her tightly in his arms while his tongue penetrated her mouth in a deep, reassuring kiss.

She was instantly transformed into simply being in the present, there with him without any further thought at all. He slowly pulled his head back and smiled into her eyes. "Hello there," he said, keeping his right arm around her. "It's wonderful to see you again. Thank you for inviting me over."

"The pleasure is all mine," she responded, snuggling up to his side to feel the fabric of his suit against her body. Her freshly shaved pussy was already tingly. "Would you like to adjourn to the living room?"

"A splendid idea, and we can crack open this bottle."

He followed her down the hallway, paying particular visual attention to her movement of her pristine white buttocks with each step she took, to where two crystal wine glasses and a bottle opener were sitting atop a small table in front of a floral couch. She smirked and spread an afghan over the seat before they sat down, then watched as Duncan opened the bottle, poured, and handed a glass to her.

"This is a particular favorite of mine," he told her. "It's a South American merlot."

Lydia first took a sip and then following Duncan's lead followed with a large mouthful. "It's delicious," she said. "And so sweet for a red wine."

Duncan stood up and started to remove his jacket. "Do you have somewhere to put this?"

"Certainly." She jumped to her feet, took his jacket to hang in the hallway closet and then stood in front of him when she promptly returned. He engaged her eyes with his while he slowly unfastened his silk tie and she felt moisture forming between her legs as he slid the tie away from his shirt collar and wrapped it around her left wrist.

Suddenly, she had her back to him and his hands were caressing her nipples before working down her arms to her wrists, wrists that were now being bound together with silk. "I'm going to have you on your knees for me," he whispered into her right ear.

Without her pussy even being touched, her legs almost gave way beneath her, and she was grateful that his strong hands were holding onto her. He eased her to the floor and positioned her knees eighteen inches apart. She watched in anticipation as he unbuckled his belt, unzipped his pants, and pulled aside his underwear to reveal his eager erection to her, which he then grasped in his right hand. "Open your mouth," he instructed while pulling back his foreskin, and when she instantly complied he slid his glistening purple bulb across her tongue. She responded by hungrily licking the pre-cum from him while his left hand moved to the back of her head. "Good girl," he told her. "Now suck."

Lydia obediently closed her lips around Duncan's stiff rod and pressed it against the roof of her mouth with her tongue as she took it halfway in. She eagerly caressed his cock with her tongue while she slid her mouth back and forth, taking him deeper each time. The vulnerability she felt in this position, on her knees with her hands tied behind her back and his hands now entwined in her hair to control the position and movement of her head, was more intoxicating than the wine. She drank Duncan's surge of nectar deeply while her glistening eyes looked upwards at the pleasure on his face that she was so happily providing for him, continuing until his ejaculation had completely subsided and he slid himself from her mouth.

"Was that my appetizer?" She asked sweetly.

"Um, hmm," Duncan nodded affirmatively as he eased her to her feet and untied her wrists. Lydia, clearly, was on the same page with him.

She remained naked as they ate the perfectly prepared salmon and capers while he sat at the table in his open necked shirt and trousers. The music of Rachmaninoff provided perfect background for their discussion about how Dostoyevsky had so deftly created characters in his books that were neither good nor bad, but a combination; much like people in real life. This paved the way for talking about Duncan's secret life and how he managed to keep it separate from what he called the 'real' world.

"It's a matter of compartmentalizing," he explained. "I'm sure you're already doing it without being conscious of it. For instance, have you told anybody at work about your desire to be a submissive?"

"Absolutely not," Lydia chuckled and finished her wine. "I see your point. Such things are best kept secret."

"But they are still a part of who you are," Duncan added. "The secret life provides you with completeness, gives you a sense of balance, without interfering with the other ninety-five percent of your life."

"And you find you can maintain that separation?"

Duncan poured the last of the wine evenly into their glasses and raised his. "Indeed," he said.

"Would you like dessert now," she asked. "Or would you prefer to wait a while?"

Duncan finished his wine, smiled and stood up. "Later," he said. "Right now I would like you to show me your bedroom."

Lydia had always had mixed feelings about her four poster princess bed. Previous boyfriends had teased her about it being overtly feminine or even childish, but even as a child she had always imagined a darker side to the fairy tale princesses. Since a prince could have any woman he wanted she reasoned that the one he chose would have to be very special indeed, and the submissive fantasies produced by her wild imagination as she stared up at the four bedposts had provided her with many masturbation scenarios over the years. She lay down on top of the bed and fought the urge to masturbate right there while she watched Duncan remove his shirt. The tie he had removed earlier was draped around the back of his neck, and while Lydia attentively watched he reached into each of his trouser pockets and slowly produced an additional tie from each of them and laid them over his shoulders. Her breathing was such that she could not close her mouth with the sudden realization that she may be entering into of one of her never spoken about fantasies.

Duncan did not disappoint. He quickly had her spread-eagled with her hands and wrists tightly bound by his silk ties, the other ends of which were each firmly attached to one the four posts. He then sat on the edge of the bed next to her and began teasing her nipples with light squeezes between his thumbs and forefingers while he descended his mouth onto hers for a ravenous, tongue engaging kiss. He squeezed her nipples harder and harder while his tongue invaded her mouth until her jaw began to quiver, then he eased back from the kiss while his hands moved into simply massaging her breasts.

"That's very good," he told her. "I'm establishing your baselines, and your nipples have a delightful tolerance level. Have you ever had them clamped?"

Lydia rapidly flipped her head from side to side while imaging what a nipple clamp might be like. "No, I haven't," she said quietly, then added, "Is that something you're going to do to me?"

"Oh, most definitely," he smiled reassuringly at her. "But not today." He then moved closer to the foot of the bed and brushed her pussy lips with his right index finger. They parted at his touch, enabling him to lubricate his fingertip with her juices before he moved it to her clitoris and lightly vibrated it. He watched her face while he rubbed her clitoris faster, then harder, until she was uncontrollably pulling against the restraints. "Let yourself go," he said, then added a second finger and rubbed her hard.

While Lydia screamed into climax he calmly eased back the pressure, but kept the two fingers in place, and stroked her engorged clit gently until her breathing was restored. "You've noticed by now that you haven't completely come back down," he told her. "A wonderful thing about a female body is its propensity for multiple orgasms. All I have to do now is keep you in this hyper-excited state, and I will be able to summon them at will."

Using fingers from both hands he then spread her pussy lips wide apart and she gasped as she felt the cool air from the overhead fan blowing between them.

"Let's visit your g-spot now, shall we?"

It was a question to which she would, of course, have no objection. Duncan's exploration of her body was providing her with such incredible arousal that as far as she was concerned he would do whatever he wanted to her. Of course, there was also the fact that she was also restrained and couldn't do anything about it anyway. It was more than her lack of control that was so exciting, though, it was that Duncan was taking care of her. She noticed how he watched her eyes and her expressions, he felt her muscles tighten, it was as if he knew precisely how she was feeling at all times, and could therefore anticipate what would most excite her next, whether it be additional tactile stimulation or the stimulation of his authoritative voice. "Please," she gasped.

Lydia's smooth pussy was wonderfully lubricated and Duncan circled her vagina with his fingers before inserting one, and then two, of them, penetrating two knuckles deep inside her. He crooked them slightly to make contact with the ridged area against the upper wall that comprised her g-spot and was delighted with how prominently raised the ridges felt against his fingertips. "You have a very nicely aroused g-spot, indeed," he told her with a borderline sadistic smile; he had control over her orgasms and was thrilled at how quickly he was able to arrive at this state with her. "So let's see how you like this," he teased, and then applied pressure and started rubbing.

Lydia's back arched off the bed as far as she could move it while her mouth opened wide into a scream of delight that was so high pitched that it was almost silent. Duncan kept his fingers inside her until she settled. "And apparently, you like it a lot."

He then lay down next to her, but kept his fingers in place. "Since I have control over your orgasms," he whispered a few inches away from her lips. "Let me demonstrate what I mean."

He began to move his fingers inside her again and she instantly began to pant. He leaned closer and gently kissed her lips. "You will cum on the count of three," he said. "One," he pressed his fingers against her g-spot.

"Two," he vibrated his fingers and began to apply pressure.

"Three," he squeezed, delighting in her instant, "Ohmigod," and the rush of hot fluid across his hand.

Duncan slowly removed his fingers; Lydia's baseline had been most successfully established. He stood up and untied her ankles, but left her wrists restrained. No longer willing to deny his own highly aroused state, he slowly unbuckled his belt while gazing at her still trembling nakedness. His clothing removed, he climbed up onto the bed, picked up her ankles and spread her legs wide apart as he positioned himself between then. "And now," he told her as he leaned forward and moved his hands to the bed on either side of her, which forced her legs to remain spread on the outside of his arms. "I'm going to fuck you."

Just those words were almost enough to bring Lydia to another climax, but it was his rigid cock pulsing deep inside her that took her over that edge. With her arms still restrained and her legs pushed up and apart she was unable to move, unable to resist; she was his for the taking, and she loved that fact that he was doing so.

3 PLEASURE-PAIN

Lydia's mind was racing with anticipation as she drove to Duncan's house. She was dressed in the three items he had told her to wear; black dress, black lace panties, black shoes, and nothing else. It pleased her that he provided such clear instructions, and she liked following them.

This was going to their third session, she believed the correct term might be scene, or was it an encounter? Could it be a date? Their previous two times together were certainly different from any other dates she had been on, and Duncan had provided her with multiple orgasms with an intensity far exceeding anything she'd ever experienced on a date before. She knew it was inappropriate to make such comparisons because he had made things clear from the outset that, for him, his world as a dominant was segmented from his real life. But she was also well aware that she had formed an emotional attachment to Duncan. It probably began before she even met him, he had been so eloquent via email that his intelligence was a given. But after they met in person and she also experienced his ability to make her feel so intensely, she'd had no choice but to fall for him.

She knew that it was silly, but she couldn't stop herself from wondering about the women who may exist in that real life of his. "Jealousy?" She asked out loud. "Absolutely not," she answered herself almost by knee-jerk. She was way too smart for that; her thinking about it was simple curiosity, that's all.

All such thoughts faded, however, as she pulled into Duncan's driveway, and by the time she excitedly stood by his front door and rang the bell they were no longer a part of her consciousness.

"I'm surprised that I'd never come across mead before I met you," Lydia said as she sank down onto the black leather couch, sitting sideways and cross legged so her right thigh was prominently exposed to him from where he was sitting across from her. "It really is delicious."

"Without mass media promotion, most people don't have the opportunity to be introduced to it," he said. "It's almost secret nature makes it the perfect drink for my secret world." He quaffed a satisfying draught. "And you are also correct that it is delicious." He smiled at her. "Now, uncross your legs and sit facing me directly."

"Like this?" She asked, sitting upright with her knees together.

"Yes, but move your legs apart and show me that you're wearing the correct panties." He nodded when the black lace came into his view. "Very good. When we are alone, your knees are never to touch while you are sitting, and you must sit so I have a clear view up your skirt or dress." He stood up to refill her mead, then sat next to her. "Unless I'm sitting beside you, of course."

She leaned against him as he put his arm around her, and remained still while he unzipped the back of her dress and kissed her neck and shoulders. Her mind was toying with the implication he had just dropped that there would be times where they might not be alone, perhaps out in public together?

Duncan took both of their wine glasses, placed them on the coffee table, and slid Lydia's dress down to her waist so that her arms were pinned in the sleeves by her sides. He then leaned her back against the couch, kissed her, and squeezed each of her nipples to erection. His sadistic smile emerged as he produced a small chain which had three clamps attached to it. "Two of these are for your nipples," he told her, leaving her imagine where the third clamp went while he carefully attached them. "And I have them on a very mild setting to begin."

Lydia couldn't quite describe how the nipple clamps felt because they produced such a combination of sensations. There was pressure, there was pulling, but there was also something else. All she knew was that she liked it.

Duncan had her stand up and he slid her dress down to her feet, then pulled the belt from his trousers and tied her hands behind her back with it. "Come," he said, and walked her around the table and stood her in front of his armchair. He sat down and admired the pose for a full minute with his legs apart, then reached out and slid her panties down and sat her on his left thigh. His left hand behind her back to steady her, he leaned over and kissed her while the fingers of his right hand aroused her clitoris.

"That's right," he whispered as he backed his mouth away from the kiss. "That is where the third clamp goes."

She gasped as he slowly eased the clamp onto her engorged clit, but he shoved his tongue into her mouth immediately afterwards and held her in that kiss until she calmed. The initial pain/pinch quickly gave way to incredible warmth and the desire for it to be touched.

"On your feet now."

Duncan stood her up and the slight tug as the chain tightened between her clitoris and nipples felt as good as sex. He then made her walk through his house, and then up the stairs where every step pulled in a different way, and stood her by the side of his bed. "Please," she stammered. "Please touch me. Please let me cum."

"Would you like to ask me properly?" He enjoyed his sadistic teasing since he had explained to her via email what the activity of 'asking properly' entailed.

Lydia immediately dropped to her knees. Duncan had told her, taught her, that when she was with him that oral was not a sex act but an act of submission, as well as a way for her to ask for favors. His allowing her to swallow would be the way in which he would communicate his approval. "Please sir," she panted with a voice close to desperation. "Please cum in my mouth."

Those are such wonderful words to hear from a submissive. Duncan leaned against the bed and quickly unfastened his pants while she nuzzled against them, and as he unzipped them she pressed her lips against the bulge in his underwear. He slipped them down and she lunged to take his erection in her mouth, bobbing her head and sucking with such a fury that he ejaculated within mere minutes, sharing an audible sigh of satisfaction with her while she sucked and swallowed to his completion. He leaned forward and kissed the top of her head, then helped her to her feet and removed the belt to free her wrists. He then scooped her up in his arms and gently placed her in the middle of his bed.

"First before you cum," he told her. "Is that you need to be held down."

Lydia noticed he was attaching Velcro straps to her wrists and ankles.

"It's called an under bed restraint system," he explained as he clipped straps to all four appendages and then tightened them so she was spread across the bed. He then licked his fingertip and touched it to the part of her engorged clitoris that was protruding above the clamp. She gasped, but his motive there was to determine her range of motion; she had none.

He then produced a vibrator, turned it on with a flourish, and lightly touched it to each nipple before pushing it under the chain so that all three clamps were simultaneously vibrating. Satisfied that she was ready, he then sat next to her spread legs and touched the vibrator against her clamped clit. All she could move was her head, and it thrashed from side to side as she approached closer and closer to climax, but right before she reached that point he pulled on the chain to snap the clamp from her clit and pushed down on it with the vibrator. It drove her wild; she looked like a bound beast railing against her bonds as successive waves of delight ravaged her body.

Lydia was almost worn out when Duncan turned the vibrator off and lay by her side. He touched her left nipple with his tongue as he eased the clamp from it, then immediately took it into his mouth and gently sucked it as the blood rushed back in. Repeating with her right side, he then dropped the chain onto the floor and kissed her. "Tired?" He asked teasingly.

"I'm exhausted, but very, very happy," she replied. "I can't believe the things you do to me."

"Then we shall adjourn to the couch for more wine and a breather."

"You're very sensual, Lydia," Duncan told her as they were cuddled together on the leather couch. "And you've been responding beautifully to being restrained." He gave her a quick kiss. "Tell me your thoughts about the clamps."

"I was a little afraid because it seemed they would hurt, and they did at first, but the pain quickly turned to being desirable and then I wanted more of it. I was most surprised by the one you put on my clit because it went so quickly from pain to pleasure." She ginned. "Was that because you had me so hot to begin with?"

Duncan grinned back at her. "With some women the proper application of pain serves to heighten heir arousal, especially with a natural submissive such as yourself."

"Are you telling me that you can put me in a state where the more pain I take, the more intense my orgasms will become? Lydia was very interested. "How do you know how far to take it?"

"By watching and paying attention to you."

"Are there limits?"

"Not so much limits, but something that I call your 'edge.' It's that teetering point where you achieve the maximum pleasure before it becomes too much." He took a thoughtful drink of his mead while watching her take in what he just said. "And it moves up over time," he added, anticipating her question.

Lydia smiled over her wine glass, then guzzled the contents and placed the empty vessel down on the tabletop. "Soo…?"

Duncan also finished his drink, and then eased her face down across his lap. He gathered her wrists in his left hand and pinned them to the couch above her head, then began spanking her bottom. "I'm going to give you a proper spanking this time," he told her.

Lydia gasped as both the heat on her bottom and the volume of the slaps intensified, but the heat was also spreading to and between her thighs and the spanking was turning her on sexually. She began to pant as tears formed in her eyes, the pleasure/pain was incredible. Was she crying? Things were becoming blurry, she couldn't tell. Suddenly the spanking ceased and she was kneeling on the floor with her upper body lying across the couch. Duncan was behind her, he was holding her hips, and he was fucking her doggy style. Faster and faster. She exploded into ecstasy and then collapsed, completely spent.

4 DATE

Lydia's nipples were tender and her clitoris was extremely sensitive to her touch when she awoke the next morning. There were bruises on her bottom, too, but she'd had so much fun getting them that she didn't mind at all. In fact, when she examined herself in the mirror she decided she liked having these 'reminders' of her time with Duncan. She loved everything about being submissive. From being told what to wear and how sit, to being tied up and spanked, it was all such an incredible turn on. The fact that she trusted Duncan to take care of her meant he could do anything he wanted with her, and she wanted him to do all of those things, whatever they might be. All she wanted was to please him, and have him pleased with her in return.

Duncan, for his part, was thrilled with his new submissive. She had a high baseline tolerance, she was clearly aroused by bondage, and the spanking he had given her had taken her to the edge of subspace. She excited him, and with the knowledge that she was ready for more he was already considering her to be his.

He also found himself thinking about her in a more traditional manner; she shared his interest in classical music and he had tickets to a concert on Saturday night. The last time he took a date to the symphony she had clapped wildly after the first movement of Beethoven's piano concerto, drawing glares from the audience and embarrassing him terribly, and the date before that had chatted incessantly instead of losing herself in the music. Since then, Duncan had been attending classical concerts alone. Lydia, however, could be the perfect symphony date. He knew it would be violating his own segmentation rules, but what harm could there be in sharing a concert they would both enjoy? He called and asked her to go with him on Saturday.

Duncan drove them to the concert and on their return to Lydia's house she sat in the passenger seat next to him with her dress up past the tops of her stockings and legs sufficiently parted for him to tease her through her panties in between his shifting gears. Since she interpreted this delightful evening to have been an actual date, and the streets leading to her house were quiet and dark this time of night, Lydia felt sufficiently emboldened to lean towards him and place her hand over the bulge in his pants. He smiled and touched his right hand to the back of her head, which was all the encouragement she needed. She immediately unzipped his pants, and by the time he pulled into her driveway her head was on his lap and she was enthusiastically performing a movement that is always an excellent finish to a classical concert, the fellatio. He turned the engine of and leaned back against the corner of the seat and the car door to allow her the freedom to continue her performance, before they went inside for coffee and chocolates.

Because Duncan had cum in her mouth in the car Lydia felt entitled to a request, so when she served his coffee she asked him, "Will you come to bed and have regular sex with me tonight?" She really wanted to ask him to make love to her but was afraid to use those words because of the reaction they might have provoked, and after such an elegant evening the use of the f-word would have clearly been inappropriate.

"But, of course," he told her as he raised the china cup to his lips and sipped his coffee. "After all, tonight was a date." He closed his right eye and immediately puzzled to himself as to why he had said such an odd thing.

"Really?" She snuggled up to him on the couch; it meant so much for her to hear that. "Does this include me as part of your real world, then, as well as your having me as your willing submissive?" Her words were laced with caution, but she couldn't suppress them.

"I'm finding those lines to be a bit blurry where you're concerned, Lydia," he answered thoughtfully. "But what I will tell you is that I very much enjoyed going to the symphony with you tonight." He leaned to kiss her, first holding his cup at arm's length so as not to spill it, but then put it down on the coffee table so he could hold her with both arms and engage in a much more interactive session. He then eased back. "Let's go to bed," he told her.

They held hands as they went upstairs and kissed profusely while undressing each other in the bedroom.

Both naked, Duncan scooped Lydia up in his arms while she wrapped her arms around his shoulders and stared adoringly into his eyes as he carried her onto the bed. Perhaps it was just conventional sex that followed, but the passion expressed in the accompanying kisses and the intensity conveyed by his body as she wrapped her legs tightly around him provided them both with a satisfaction that neither had experienced from the missionary position before.

Duncan left around 5am, needing to get home and change before heading to his office, and Lydia stayed up after she saw him off and put the kettle on; it was only an hour before she was usually up for work anyway.

She curled up into her favorite chair with a cup of hot tea and thought back about the wonderful time they had shared. In addition to being the perfect dominant Duncan was also a wonderful lover, but now permutations of that oh so powerful l-word were causing her consternation. If she were to speak of love, even if it just became a topic of discussion, it would probably chase him away and she would lose him completely from both of his worlds. There was safety and simplicity in the world of being his submissive because their roles were clearly defined, but the real world was a messy place. Both of them were survivors of failed marriages, something neither of them would ever consider entering into again, so she understood his stated distain for committed relationships and the reason that he considered dating to merely be a casual activity, more of a sport or a hobby than anything that would affect him emotionally or impact on his lifestyle.

Lydia wished she was able to segment her life as Duncan did, but she had no such control and her feelings for him occupied her entire being. It scared her that increasing levels of submission would only enhance her love for him, but the compulsion of her need to submit to him overrode that fear. Was she just being a hopeless romantic in thinking that she might be able to straddle his barrier and thus be able to provide him with satisfaction in both parts of his life?

5 SUBSPACE

Duncan sat at his desk with a mug of coffee and reflected on the previous night. It had been wonderful to go on a date with a woman who not only enjoyed the symphony but who also engaged in intelligent conversation with him about it afterwards. The sex had been good too, at least as good as any other date he had been on in recent years. Real world Lydia was intelligent and charming, someone he could pretty much take anywhere and be comfortable that she wouldn't embarrass him. It was too bad that he had not met her in a real world context. He was feeling very uncomfortable at how he had stupidly muddied the waters like this.

Duncan drained his coffee and poured another while pursuing this train of thought. His primary interest in Lydia was as his submissive, so why had he taken her into his real world in the first place? The world at large was full of potential women for him to date, but a natural submissive who seemed so in tune with him was a rare find, indeed. Putting her in both of his worlds could detract from, or even ruin, the potentially perfect dominant-submissive relationship that he and Lydia were embarking on. He gulped his coffee while continuing his pondering; the logical solution would obviously be to avoid any more date-like situations and so restore the proper focus. He plunked his mug onto the top of his desk and resolved that all future encounters with Lydia would take place at his house, and to ensure that times with her remained where they belonged he would have no more conventional sex with her.

Now that she knew how bondage increased the intensity of her physical responses, Lydia expressed great interest when Duncan emailed her of his desire to restrain her even more the next time they met. He also told her that they would be further exploring that delightful intersection of pleasure and pain, and that he was going to be introducing her to a flogger. The mixed thoughts these emails had produced were rampaging through her brain as she drove towards his house, but they suddenly fell quiet as she parked in his driveway. She was again entering Duncan's secret world as his submissive, and by the time she rang the doorbell her only thought was one of anticipation.

He closed the door behind her after she entered the foyer and immediately lifted her dress up and over her head. As instructed, she was wearing nothing underneath. "Kick of your shoes," he said as he hung her dress in the hallway closet, and then turned around and wrapped a leather band around her right wrist. She stared at it as he secured the buckle; it was decorated with a row of metal studs and it had a metal loop firmly attached. He then attached another to her left wrist before ordering her to sit on the steps so he could also put similar leather cuffs around her ankles.

In hopes of having him express pleasure with her she sat with her legs spread and arms to her sides which gave him full view of her breasts and genitalia, but he remained expressionless while he fastened the buckles.

"We're going upstairs now," he told her as he helped her to her feet and then silently followed behind her as she ascended. There were two black leather floggers lying on the bed, one was about a yard long while the other was half that size. Duncan picked the larger one up. "This one is for your back," he said as he gently swayed it back and forth while letting the implication of what the other might be for sink in before adding, "So I want you face down on the bed."

Lydia climbed up onto the bed and lay face down while Duncan quickly snapped the straps of the restraint system to each of the four buckle loops, then walked around the bed tightening them to stretch her into being completely spread-eagled and immobilized. She sensed that he was standing to the side of her as she felt the soft leather tails of the flogger drape across her bottom and the inside of her thighs and then slide up across her back and off her shoulders.

"I'm going to use this flogger to warm up your shoulders and your bottom," he told her. "But we'll begin lightly."

The first thud preceded sensation, and the subsequent combination of sound with impact of the leather tails on her shoulders was pure pleasure, it was rather akin to a firm massage. She involuntarily emitted a purring 'mmm' sound, which prompted Duncan to stop and move to the foot of the bed.

"Now for your bottom."

The sound was different, but the first few landings of the flogger on either side of her buttocks felt as delightful as those on her upper back. However, Duncan then increased the intensity and she began to flinch and pull against the restraints. Her bottom suddenly felt like it was glowing and she was panting, but she was at a loss about how to interpret the curious reaction her body was having to the flogging. Duncan administered a final stroke to each buttock and when she felt his fingers move in between her legs she realized how incredibly wet she was. He easily shoved two, then three, fingers inside her and proceeded to apply her moisture to her hot bottom, using it like a salve. She gasped each time his fingers returned for more but she was unable to squirm sufficiently to cause them to brush against her inflamed clitoris.

Duncan was delightedly aware of Lydia's state of arousal. He lay on the bed next to her, kissed the nape of her neck, and whispered, "Now I'm going to turn you over," into her right ear while he reached over to unclip the wrist restraint. He then slid off the bed and quickly unsnapped the other three, told her to roll over onto her back, then immediately reattached the clips to her ankles so her legs were again spread wide apart. He then clipped the wristbands together and attached them to the headboard before producing a blindfold, which he slid over the top of her head while telling her, "You'll enjoy it even more like this." He then picked up the smaller flogger.

Duncan began slowly with her breasts until the firmness of her nipples and the fact she was breathing through an open mouth suggested that she was ready. "Did you know that this small flogger is also called a pussy flogger?" He asked teasingly, rhetorically, as he draped the tassels across her twitching labia lips before beginning his gentle administration. It took only a few minutes of increasing intensity before her pussy was wonderfully red and engorged and her now prominent clitoris was begging him to ensure that the tails of the flogger made direct contact with each stroke. He watched her mouth open wider with each breath she took until he surmised that she was on the verge of reaching orgasm, so then stopped with the flogging and positioned his right index finger onto her clitoris. He had much better control with his fingers. "We're going to keep you at your edge for a while," he told her, then patted her pussy. "In fact, we're going to move it up a notch."

He then slapped her pussy in an upward motion with the fingers of his right hand, producing the desired gasping from Lydia, and continued until her upper row of teeth began to bite into her lower lip, whereupon he immediately stopped and soothed her clitoris with his fingertips. Within fifteen seconds she was again about to explode into orgasm, but he resumed the pussy spanking which prevented the progression and kept her held in that 'almost' state. This time, however, there was no flinching of her lips; she had transitioned from pain-pleasure to pure pleasure. Duncan kept his hand on top of her hot clit while he slid the blindfold away from her eyes. He wanted to watch her entire face as he proceeded to rub her clitoris to full orgasm and deliver her into subspace.

Lydia's impassioned screams of ecstasy were the loudest Duncan had ever heard and the back and forth thrashing of her head as he brought her into continuous waves again and again had him so hard that his cock began to hurt as it strained to be released form the confines of his pants. He eased back the motion of his right hand, settling Lydia into a state of almost unconscious bliss, and quickly unbuckled her restraints. She remained motionless and smiling at him while he took off his clothes and lay down next to her and held her. He needed release and wanted so badly to fuck her, but was determined not to cave in and have vaginal sex with her. Her mouth would be useless for sucking while she was in this condition, and while his cock would be satisfied with deep throating her, he wanted to hold her and be on top of her when he came. There was only one solution, so he rolled her onto her side and pressed his body against her back. He took her hot buttocks in his hands and slid his cock between them, rubbing the pre-cum from his excited bulb against her anal opening. Her body responded positively and the gentle rocking of her hips soon encouraged his penetration of her butt. The tightness of her sphincter squeezing his rod as he pushed it into her drove him wild and he rolled her onto her front and began to almost selfishly pound into her. This position ground Lydia's clit into the sheet and caused her compliant body to enter into one more orgasmic frenzy as Duncan held her face down with his body while he ejaculated his cum deep inside her and exhaled a deep sigh of satisfaction onto the back of her head.

Spent, he lay on top of her for several minutes before he slid off, rolled her to face him, and held her tightly, silently, for over an hour. When she once again became animated and able to use her mouth for words in addition to her huge smile, she simply exclaimed, "Wow," and threw her arms around him.

They then went downstairs for cake and tea.

"Everything is a bit of a blur from the time you put the blindfold on me," Lydia told him. "I mean, I was aware of what you were doing but I was in such a state of pure pleasure that my body just did whatever you wanted it to. And every time you did something it felt so good, and I came so many times, that I think I just got so worn out that I must have dozed off while you were holding me. Was that subspace?"

"Indeed it was, and I also satisfied myself with your body once I had you there."

"And I am so very pleased that you did. That was

the first time that you ever completely let yourself go with me, and I want you to know that I loved it." She smirked. "And you can cum up my ass, or in my mouth, or any other way you want me any time you like." Lydia wanted to say so much more, but instead she just cuddled up to him.

6 FINDING DEFINITION

Relationships with other people had always posed a quandary for Duncan. As Jean Paul Sartre so eloquently put it, the knowledge that we are free to make our own choices in life creates anxiety within us because we are also influenced by what other people may think of those choices. The common response of most people is to therefore deny their own freedom and not do the things they want. Duncan knew that if the world at large knew of his dominant, what they would consider deviant, sexual proclivities they would condemn him for it and he would lose his standing in the community, and his business, and therefore the income he relied upon, would no doubt fail. Such was the reason that Duncan had chosen to segment out a part of his life;

a secret world where he could be his authentic self, while still ensuring a cash flow to live on.

Lydia was without doubt the ideal submissive for his secret, compartmentalized world, and he was thrilled as he imagined the activities that they would be indulging in as they moved forward. So why was his brain now messing with this perfect relationship? Why did he want to so badly to include her in his real world, to have conventional sex with her, to have her join him in the things he liked to do which were outside the realm of dominance and submission?

It was obvious that his blunder had been in taking her to the symphony and then having vaginal sex with her; it had provoked an emotional response. Had it also done the same with her? Was this damage irreparable? There was a high probability that this emotional genie was not going to willingly return to its bottle, but he had to try. He invited Lydia to dinner at his house with the full intent to discuss this with her in an attempt to restore the purity of their dominant-submissive relationship.

Lydia eagerly accepted his invitation because she too wanted to discuss, or more importantly define, just what their relationship was all about. Rather than run the risk of losing Duncan she was willing to keep her emotions to herself and share only her physical feelings with him. However, their date had suggested he may also have feelings for her, and the fact that he had avoided any discussion in that regard the last time they were together had ignited a hope in her that their relationship could be more. She would tread carefully, and if it turned out that he only wanted her for the segmented part of his life, then so be it. She would at least make the 5% of his life that he devoted to D/s the best it could possibly be, and he would never need to know how so much of her life was impacted by his presence in it.

With Tchaikovsky playing in the background and a centerpiece of a perfectly roasted rack of lamb between two flickering candles, the stage was set for Duncan to initiate the conversation which he imagined was going to be just about Lydia's submissiveness. "Have you told your friends or people that you work with about what we like to do?" He asked as he poured a glass of cabernet.

"Not at all," she replied. "Like you, I'm keeping that part of my life a close secret." She took a sip of wine. "Unlike you, though, I do think about it all of the time and as a result I haven't wanted to be with anyone else since we've been seeing each other."

"That doesn't sound healthy; I wouldn't want our relationship to be taking anything away from your regular life. "

"Oh, it doesn't at all. In fact, the time I spend with you completely fills that need for me."

"But surely it should be adding something to your life."

"Believe me, time with you adds tremendously to my life. Simone de Beauvoir said that sexual pleasure in a woman is a kind of magic requiring complete abandon, and until I met you I never quite understood what she was talking about. Based on that, I think she may have been a submissive too."

"You read de Beauvoir?" Duncan was impressed.

"Oh yes, in fact I rather like all of the existentialists."

The unthinkable flooded into Duncan's brain. They had so much in common, was it really possible that all of this could exist for him in a single person? He realized they had finished eating and suggested, "Let's continue the wine, and our conversation, on the couch."

They rose from the table but before they left for the living room Duncan took Lydia in a firm embrace and kissed her, then in an attempt to refocus himself on just his dominant role he ordered her to strip.

She cheerfully complied, carefully laying her clothes over the back of the dining room chair, and then seductively walking naked to the couch while Duncan followed carrying the refilled wine glasses. Her pristine bottom was in desperate need of added color, and it was his intention to put her across his lap and provide her with a sound spanking, followed by sliding her onto the floor where he would hold her head and make her take him in her mouth. But when he sat down next to her his plan was overridden by an unshakable thought in his head, and instead of spanking her he found himself asking her a question, rephrasing what she had told him earlier. "So you really are not dating anybody in the real world, then?"

"No," she said demurely as she took a sip of wine.

While Lydia's confirmation that there were no other men in her life inwardly delighted Duncan, it underscored how he had lost control of the conversation and he desperately pressed to turn it back around towards into his comfort zone. "But doesn't that mean our relationship is causing you to make choices that you otherwise wouldn't make?" His tone had become professorial. "The existentialists would have a field day with your letting another's influence take that freedom away from you, you know."

"Not at all, because those are choices that I'm freely making," she smiled at him. "I don't have your ability to segment, Duncan." She drank some wine, but then as she leaned to put the glass on the table she looked away from him and added, "But that doesn't mean you're not free to carry on as you always have. I know it's easy for you."

Duncan stared at the side of her pretty face, her firm breasts, and those delightful naked thighs. "Easy?" He thought to himself. If only she knew the torment he had been wrestling with these past few days.

He turned her to face him and gazed deeply into her eyes while allowing her to read his. Rather than simplifying his relationship with Lydia, the evening had instead brought into focus the strength of his emotional connection to her, and he suddenly had the need to share that with her. He scooped her up in his arms and positioned her on his lap to hold her. Everything they had been talking about coalesced in his brain as he realized there was no need for a secret world where Lydia was concerned. She was so special that she belonged in his entire world.

Duncan carried Lydia to his bed where he spent the rest of the night making love to her. Going forward, she was going to be the de Beauvoir to his Sartre.

ABOUT RONDA DEMURE

Ronda DeMure's stories of submission and dominance are both sensual as well as sexual. The author pays close attention to the immersive experience of D/s, which involves both the psychological and the physiological aspects of submission and domination, in order to provide a truly erotic experience for her readers.

On the web: https://submissionanddominance.com